Halloweenland

A

Fairy Tale Detective

Mystery

By

Spike Brown

Illustrations by
Sharon Maynard Burrows

Tower Bridge Books

For Janet & Clive Rutherford

of Daylesford

This is a fun, spooky book, creepy and entertaining. It involves a young girl who visits a remote hamlet whose inhabitants are haunted by pumpkin-headed creatures every Halloween night. These creatures often take the form of ordinary people, only to dispel their disguise and show their true appearance. I highly recommend this book.

RATING: *****

I really enjoyed reading this book. I felt like I had jumped back in time to the great adventures of our youth solving mysteries. Thank you for a great read.

RATING: *****

CHAPTER

1

The Portal

Betty arrived at the train station in Arundel to begin the last leg of her journey to a small, remote village, not much bigger than a hamlet, between Pulborough and the forested area of Bog Common.

There was a bit of time before the train came in and, sitting on the platform bench, she overheard the porter speaking in hushed tones to the stationmaster.

"Swarms of ghosts have been seen in the village churchyard — more than usual."

"Well, Olaf, the train is in, best load the girl's luggage — an increase in the ghost population you say, listen carefully. The girl has special abilities and must be allowed to pass, change the points and open the tunnel up — the portal is now energised."

After travelling from Glim Glumswick, with the benefit of a fast, efficient and comfortable train, Betty was surprised to find the trains running forwards from Pulborough were somewhat antiquated, being hauled by wood-burning locomotives.

"Hello," said a slender girl with blonde hair who seemed to appear out of nowhere, "My name's Katrina."

She smoothed her dress over her knees. "Hello," said Betty, passing over a bag of lemon sherbets and offering her a sweet. "Want one?"

"No thanks. Have you come far?"

"Er... Glim Glumswick."

"Oh my, is this your first trip to our beautiful forest?"

"Yes."

As the train rattled along, the autumnal light was fading fast and the view from the carriage window of trees whizzing past became more and more of a gas-lit, liquidy reflection of the girl's face in the glass. Katrina prattled on, as some girls do, and Betty chomped most of the lemon sherbets. But when the train was winding its way along the forest floor, about to enter a short section of tunnel, an odd thing happened.

The gas jet in the crystal glass lamp dimmed above Katrina's head, as with a stab of horror, in the dark, flickering light, Betty saw Katrina's face transformed from being pretty into something ugly and malignant. A wide apart, oversized mouth full of large, jagged teeth, ideal for tearing flesh.

Once out of the tunnel, Katrina became herself again.

The train rounded the curve by the signal box and entered the station. Betty was glad to get out of the compartment but was polite and acted as though nothing had happened.

"Goodbye, Katrina," she said cordially.

"Goodbye — be careful. I hear there are lots of ghosts everywhere," she laughed, kicking her clumpy shoes against the compartment seat. "Them and a bunch of loopy stray dogs."

CHAPTER

Herr Bauer, from the Inn, smoking a big meerschaum pipe, was there to greet Betty on the platform.

"We are experiencing a momentous eclipse, the pumpkin moon passed in front of the other hence it's already dark." said Herr Bauer, receiving the girl's bags from the porter. "Shame, our forest looks wonderful in autumn colours."

Making their way up the cobbled street, with lamps burning brightly, the jovial innkeeper talked of the merits of

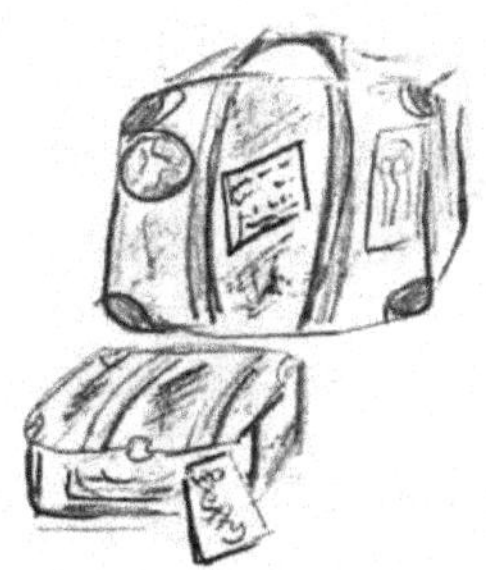

English fish and chips and asked how her journey had been. The inn, its latticed windows ablaze with lamplight, looked cheery and welcoming, despite the gruesomely painted inn sign dangling from its squeaky iron brackets above the door, that hinted of a historic place of execution nearby:

The Block & Stake

Introductions were made. Netta, it turned out, was the innkeeper's wife: Frauleins Lottie and Hildegard served behind the bar. Betty was told this remote village – was affectionately known locally as 'Heidelberger' – she supposed that having moved from Germany they had kept many of their traditions, a glimpse of a Bavarian idyl nestled into southern England. 'Pumpkin eclipse, now that's a first,' she thought, certainly a rarity for astronomers… 'must be.'

A small crowd of friendly regulars were sitting drinking steins of beer in front of a large carved stone fireplace, with logs crackling in the grate.

As a flurry of sparks spat out over the tufty hearthrug, merry laughter was to be heard amongst the clink of glasses. The evening passing pleasantly.

Betty was shown her room upstairs as well as the bathroom and loo along the landing, but once back downstairs, a brief altercation took place that was to leave a fundamental impression.

Herr Bauer was showing off his hunting gun, which was displayed on hooks above the fireplace, when Netta gleefully returned from the beer garden, clutching a small wicker basket. About to go into the kitchen, she hesitated, parting aside some bunches of winter greens.

"See, Willi, look what a prize I found growing in

the vegetable patch. When hollowed out, it will make a pretty little lamp and our kitchen shall soon be sweetened by its warm, rich smell when I bake a pie."

"Never!" screamed Herr Bauer, snatching the modestly sized pumpkin from her basket and hurling it out of the inn door in a fit of rage.

It landed with a dull splat outside. "I will not have that ... that *thing* in my inn!"

Betty was puzzled by the innkeeper's stormy outburst.

"You know All Hallows is nearly upon us, what on earth provoked you to such heights of foolishness?" shouted Herr Bauer.

"What harm can there be? It's only a small one."

"So, what happened to Klaus, Manfred, Herman, Joanna, Heinz and Frederik last October was merely light comedy? A farce?"

"No, no, Willi, forgive me. I only meant to cook a little ..."

Netta rushed up the staircase in floods of tears, her sobs could be heard from her room upstairs.

"You silly blockhead!" the innkeeper shouted despairingly at the ceiling. "Do you want us all murdered in our beds? Really, woman, whatever next."

Herr Bauer shook his head and disappeared into the kitchen to prepare a supper of roast boar and chips for Betty.

While Betty ate her supper in the convivial little restaurant, the innkeeper recounted the time he had visited London and all the sights as a young boy. The meal was delicious.

"Herr Bauer," Betty asked between mouthfuls, stabbing at her juicy steak with a fork. "Whatever happened earlier with Netta?"

"A spat – how do you English put it? A man and

wife will argue over the silliest things. I lost my temper with Netta over a trivial matter concerning an autumnal squash."

"A pump ...?"

"More lemonade?" the innkeeper interrupted, upending the jug and filling Betty's glass to the brim.

"Thank you, Herr Bauer, but the pumpkin is carved and used for decoration – not to be shunned."

"Not in our village," the innkeeper scowled. "In our village such folly would put our very lives in danger. Anyhow," he sighed, "let's change the subject. There seems no reason why your stay with us in Heidelberger should not be both pleasant and productive. I must introduce you to Professor Van Selsing, an eminent man of letters who has spent many years documenting the local history of our village. He is also our foremost authority on vampires and werewolves and other supernatural phenomena. The books he has written are quite fascinating, but I fear you young English girls are more interested in pteridomania – a fascination for collecting ferns – and crystal gazing, the past has little meaning!"

Betty politely agreed, but she *had* once stumbled on a secondhand bookshop in Wellingford stuffed full of dusty old books on witchcraft and ghosts.

She couldn't wait to meet the professor, but first she had to get something that had been bugging her off her chest.

"May I have your complete confidence, Herr Bauer?"

"Of course, m'girl."

"I travelled into that railway tunnel coming over here on the train – just me and my bag of sweets."

"Go on."

"So suddenly there's Katrina. Great crackerjack! As we are talking her face started swelling bigger and bigger."

"Is that so?"

The innkeeper took out his pipe of a carved meerschaum variety and, tamping some strands of tobacco lit the bowl, savouring the smoke as it curled up to the oak-beamed ceiling.

"Yes, into a squash – excuse me – PUMPKIN with hideous teeth. It was only a glimpse, but pretty scary."

"You really saw this?"

"I did."

"You're not fibbing?"

"No!" exclaimed Betty.

"My dear young lady!" Tears were welling up in the innkeeper's eyes. He seized both Betty's hands, overwhelmed with emotion. "You've no idea what a relief this is to me. You will not now, I trust, think of me, or any of us for that matter, as – how do you English put it – 'loonybins' when I tell you our village is cursed."

"Cursed?"

"From long ago, God knows how many eons back, but each Halloween they come from the forest to claim more of us."

"They?"

"The pumpkinheads."

A shadowy shape – round, like a football – passed the lounge bar window and Betty watched, intrigued, as the

innkeeper tip-toed across the room to fetch his hunting gun from the hooks on the wall above the fireplace, pulled back both hammers and aimed at the door. But it was a false alarm — a trick of the light — for it was only a local character called 'Old Adolf', who narrowly missed getting his head blown off.

He was one of the regulars, come to enjoy a stein of beer and a chat and gossip by the fire. The gun was hastily rehung, and the fellow welcomed. 'Old Adolf' was a retired woodcutter who lived in a tumble-down cottage on the outskirts of Heidelberger. His wrinkled, leathery skin spoke of a lifetime spent outdoors.

"I am cooking up such a pie, Willi." Netta was timidly peeping round the kitchen door, showing everybody her floury fingers. "It is fleshy and succulent to eat."

Herr Bauer looked at her coldly, he had still not forgiven his wife for her earlier transgression.

"Pie? Tell me more about this pie," said Old Adolf, drool running down his stubbly chin, for he was hungry and wished to sample a portion.

"A turnip pie," Netta explained, desperate to get back into her husband's good books for, as Lottie was fond of saying, 'the way to a man's heart is through his stomach'.

"Thank the Lord for that," said Herr Bauer, somewhat pacified. "We have a plentiful supply of winter vegetables in store, anyhow." He relit his pipe.

"A large slice for me!" Old Adolf raised his foaming stein in a toast to Netta's cooking skills.

All the while Betty was aware of a curious feeling that someone, or something from the outside, was looking in.

CHAPTER

Jacob Albert Van Selsing, using a small brass telescope, peered out of the window of his library. The pumpkin eclipse had now passed, a full moon bright and wondrous allowed to shine unhindered. He lived in an attractive Bavarian-style chalet on the outskirts of Heidelberger, within easy walking distance of the Block and Stake. It was from here, at his beloved 'Thorkierkegaard', that he organised his busy life and wrote his books. But back to that full moon... The professor was aware of how its supposedly benign radiance could affect both lunatics and animals in curious ways.

Indeed, his own research had led him to the spectacular unearthing of a skull belonging to a village idiot who had died over 300 years ago and was famed for his hairiness, big teeth and odd behaviour on the night of the full moon.

The dug-up jawbone showed all the signs of chronic mutation, being filled with a ferocious set of incisors and sharp

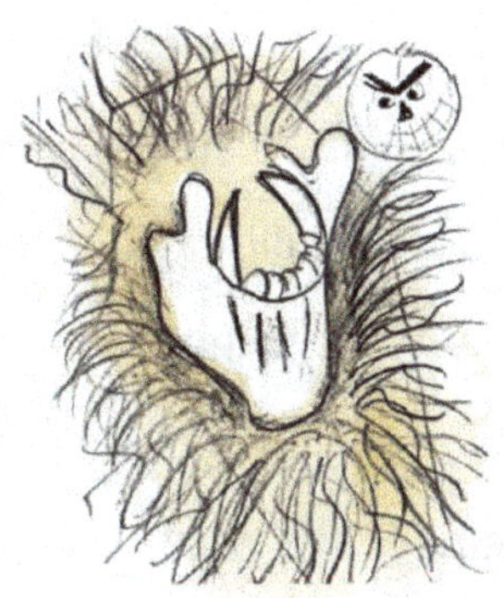

fangs, easily capable of tearing through flesh and bone.

But more remarkably, inside the preserved lead coffin, the corpse had, at some stage of decomposition, shed a pelt of thickly matted fur, and when analysed, fibres were found to be directly traceable to the wolf family.

If only all genetic mutations were quite so simple to quantify! Pumpkinheads, on the other hand, were an enigma. They seemed to exist only in this region. There was no known reference to them in any old myths, legends, folklore or fairytale literature.

But one thing was certain – they would be back this year, and not one person in the village was safe. Mein Gott, what was the date? October 30th?

Halloween Nacht was almost upon them! There was so little time.

Van Selsing abandoned his moongazing, adjusted the lamp on his desk, which shone the brighter, casting shadows over his papers and books. Picking a clay pipe from the rack, he filled it with 'Weber Tabak' and struck a match. The cursed sound of baying dogs filled his ears – and heart – with dread.

Was the full moon a factor here? Not really, because the dogs had been behaving strangely – like wolves – for a week now, and they kept up their howling well into the night, full moon or not, so something quite separate was motivating their behaviour.

The dogs seemed to sense something bad was about to happen – and they'd be right, something always happened at Halloween. It had done so for as long as he could remember, and no one had the faintest clue how to avoid it.

The professor puffed on his clay pipe, gazing in a bewildered, morose way out of the window until he noticed a torn scrap of paper pinned to the blotter, which made him refocus.

My dear Jacob

As you know, I am collecting a young lady named Betty Zmunx from the station. You'll meet her tonight at the inn.

Affectionately, Willi Bauer

He was convinced the long boarded up, weed infested abandoned railway tunnel at the end of the cutting was a portal. Whenever it opened, only one train in the years cycle ever passed through, and that normally empty, not one single passenger on board, but now... this Halloween.

Warming to the thought of his nightly trip to the Block and Stake Inn for a good dinner and pleasant conversation, Van Selsing's mind returned to the problem at hand.

The leprechaun could be traced to Ireland, the vampire to Transylvania, the boggart to Scotland – no problem. These supernatural creatures were well documented. It was easy to obtain a book or two on the subject that gave some explanation and history. Not so though the elusive pumpkinheads.

He, Jacob Van Selsing, an eminent man of letters, author of several books, who was ideally placed at the centre of this maelstrom, had not even enough factual data to write a single chapter, and this infuriated him.

He laid down his pipe in silence, and once more scoured the shelves of his library for a smidgen of information but could find nothing and was relieved when the cuckoo clock sang and whistled, for it was time for his evening stroll.

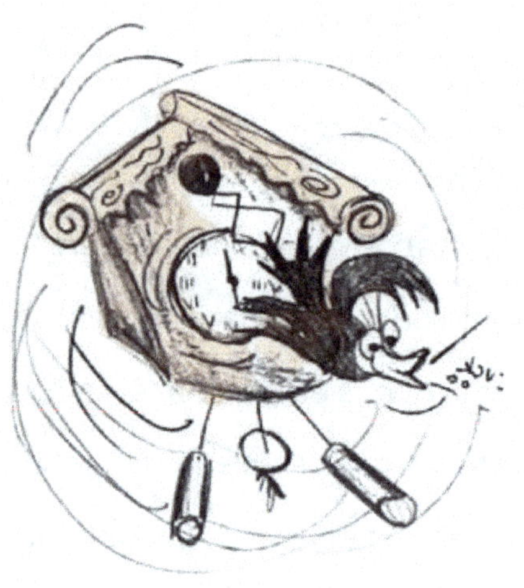

The inn door swung open, and all eyes turned to see a giant of a man – brandishing a

knobbly walking stick, wearing a wide-brimmed hat and swirling cape – enter the drinking parlour.

"Hogburger and my usual glass of Schnapps," he called out to Lottie, hanging up his hat and coming over to the fire to warm his hands.

"Good evening, Herr Professor," said the innkeeper, getting up to receive his esteemed guest. "You have not met any pumpkinheads walking over here?" This was said more in jest than literally. Herr Bauer filled the professor's glass liberally and made sure his friend was comfortably seated by the fire.

"Only the curious eyes of slavering dogs," Van Selsing replied, with obvious unease. "They peer at one through the bushes, which is most disconcerting. There is, I suspect, a pack of them congregating about the village."

"Stray dogs!" shrieked Lottie. "Why are they here? What do they want?"

"Put a sock in it, young lady," Herr Bauer called out, pulling up a chair to the hearth.

"You know, Willi, it's exasperating," continued Van Selsing, placing his cigar case on the table. "I have consulted many rare and ancient volumes yet can find no reference that a connection exists between the dogs, those stray packs of wild scavengers, and these pumpkin-headed creatures. But they sense something. Why else would they intrude upon our hamlet?"

"Good eating?"

"Eh?"

"Netta's turnip pie," chuckled Old Adolf, stretching his legs and warming the worn soles of his old boots on the brass fender. "But seriously, my dear Professor, I have never myself encountered one of these so-called pumpkinheads on All Hallows Eve, and frankly, have no intention of ever doing so. My advice, for what it's worth in this age, is, on October 31st, stay at home, lock all doors and windows and retire to bed, after a keg of the best Weizenbier beer, to read the family Bible until dawn. That offers protection, I'm sure of it. A statue of the Holy Mother, or a crucifix placed outside the door will likewise see them off."

"And you practise what you preach?" asked the professor doubtfully.

"Certainly!"

"Well, for vampires your scheme would work admirably with, perhaps, the small addition of garlic flowers, but for pumpkinheads I am not so sure."

Once Old Adolf, at the Block and Stake, got going there was no stopping him. He drank deeply from his beer stein and more revelations were forthcoming.

"Folk from the village go missing at Halloween," he emphasised, wagging his finger,  "Rumour has it these pumpkin creatures eat roasted or baked children and old folks with horseradish - and turn the other victims aged between fourteen to sixty years into mutants who on witches' night come and hassle everybody — n'more than a purge. They could be classed as ..."

"Half-human?" said Betty, wondering what her schoolmates back at Glim Glumswick would make of all this. Was there any reference to pumpkinheads in the 'supernatural' and 'unusual phenomena' books in her local library? She wondered if her friend, Professor Lallington, might know.

"Half-gourd?" suggested Lottie, joining in.

"Carnivorous pumpkins." The old ex-woodcutter was more to the point. "The Professor here tells me the pumpkinheads are creatures that will bite you and turn you into one of them, and so multiply."

"Bravo. Anything new?" asked Herr Bauer.

Betty spoke up. "Has it crossed any of your minds that the forest railway might have something to do with this?"

"The railway has served our woodland community since 1862, whatever put such a vacuous idea into your head, Betty?" expressed Herr Bauer, with a puzzled look.

"The railway's staff seemed to have such perfectly round heads."

The innkeeper laughed raucously. "What childish

trivia. Next, you'll be accusing me of being 'pumpkinised'! More Schnapps, Professor? steak, perhaps?"

"Wait," said the venerable man of letters, holding out his glass. "The young lady may have a valid point. Are you meaning to tell us the railway has had dark dealings in the past?"

"I'm meaning to say the pumpkinheads regularly travel on it," said Betty. "Take Katrina von Blaufelt, for example. Well, she was sitting opposite me in the train compartment – scary. She was bound for that next stop, what's it called - 'Heidelwagner'?"

"Well," sighed Van Selsing, wearied by his long hours of literary research and desperate to do something practical, "I suggest Willi and me, along with young Miss Zmunx here, take a trek to Heidelwagner station and see if we can turn up anything. No trains are running now because it's late, but we can walk it."

"Halloween falls tomorrow, so let's get going," said Betty excitedly.

"Our journey into the forest interior will require plenty of sustenance. Netta," Herr Bauer called out to the busy kitchen, "prepare some pocket flasks of coffee. Pack thick slices of pie and plenty of boiled eggs into my haversack – we will be leaving shortly."

"Why, where are you going at this time of night?" asked the harassed housewife, pulling on her asbestos oven gloves, stooping down low to open the oven door with its heat almost scorching her face.

"Heidelwagner. We have business to attend there concerning these swine pumpkinheads, not a word to anyone, mind. You will be left in sole charge until my return."

"Of course, dearest. Whatever you say. The pie is now freshly baked and the crust browned and crispy.

Can you smell it, Willi?"

"Yes, yes. Delicious, I'm sure. Now just get on with it, woman."

"Cut me a large slice too!" said Old Adolf, giving the fire a poke and watching the flames roar up the chimney. "Don't let those intrepid travellers hog the lot."

CHAPTER

5

Betty's Hike

The pack of feral dogs were following the trio's every step, their baleful eyes peeping from the undergrowth. Snarling, with fangs bared, they plodded stealthily beside the forest path leading to the tiny village on the outskirts of Bog Common — locally known as 'Heidelwagner' —

keeping well out of sight, but a constant presence nonetheless, their particular brand of menace masking that of something more spectral in nature.

There was a distinct nip in the air, and the carpet of pine needles and decaying autumn leaves crackled underfoot due to frost. An hour or so into the journey, Herr Bauer shone his torch into a wooded clearing, and beyond the firs could be seen the glow of lamps peeping through slats of shuttered windows in distant houses.

"Heidelwagner village," he said, as they gathered round. "But it's the station we want." He swivelled his torch round, the bright beam of light revealing a steep, earthy bank riddled with gnarled and twisted tree roots that led down to the railway line. Using the root systems as convenient footholds, they clambered down onto the track and followed the gleaming rails round to the station, stepping from sleeper to sleeper.

When they reached the darkened platforms, no lamps were lit, and the place was deserted of public wayfarers and station staff. The railway terminated here, and the line went no further.

The station included a goods yard with a siding leading to an engine shed. The yard had bunkers well-stocked with cut logs, and there was a water tower.

"Hark at those wild dogs," said Herr Bauer, no worse for the exercise. He lit his pipe with his lighter. "Should have brought my gun," he confided, a wisp a smoke seeping from the corner of his mouth.

"Aha!" Exclaimed the silver-haired professor, taking off his hat and pausing to take bearings. "I think a visit to the engine shed is in order. They may be hiding something in there."

"Tons and tons of growing compost," laughed the

innkeeper.

Betty buttoned up her fur-collared coat with a shiver against the cold autumn chill, following the others across the points to where they could trudge up the siding. Had she seen a trace of the shape of a head fade fast beyond a bush?

It would normally have taken a couple of minutes to work out how to open the shed doors, but they were already unlocked. When the doors slid across on their little, well- greased wheels, they were in for a surprise.

The gloomy interior of the shed was musty with stale old smoke. Plump, beady-eyed rats scurried along the floor, nosing about amongst the ironwork.

Everyone was staring at a pair of stationary wood-burning locomotives. A vision unveiled by the moonlight shimmering through the shed's only grubby window almost caused the innkeeper to

scream out, for he glimpsed two horrible faces superimposed on the smoke-box doors.

"Spook engines," said the shocked Willi Bauer, rubbing his eyes, seeing there was nothing there after all.

"Not spooks, exactly, Willi, but just look at the name plates."

The professor leaned a little too close so that he was touching one of the locomotives named *Tankenginestein*. He received an electric shock so nasty it made him jump back, causing his hair to stand on end for a few seconds.

"You little swine!" Van Selsing lost his temper and felt like kicking the thing, but he wisely backed off, nursing his sore fingers.

"You know," remembered Betty, "the locomotive that hauled the train I caught when I first arrived at Heidelberger was called 'Ygor'."

"Names like *Ygor* and *Tankenginestein* conjure up monsters, old keeps and haunted castles," Van Selsing said, trying to brush excess static off his sleeve. "Gotten unt Himmel! Maybe we're onto something here."

The noise of a train approaching the station along

the main line made everyone scurry to get the shed doors closed again – the pack of dogs howling menacingly from the trees up in the forest.

"Go back to Bog Common, why don't you?" So annoyed was Herr Bauer that he accidentally blew when he should have sucked, causing a flurry of sparks from his pipe that nearly set his hair alight.

The train did not take a turn up the siding to the goods yard but shunted into the station platform. The puffing engine hauled behind it the standard luggage coach and carriages, but coupled on the end was a flat wagon, and tethered to this was something truly extraordinary – it was big, round and glowed in the dark!

Then something else whizzed low overhead, only Zmunxy knew of course... it was her mate Tudor Sefton, the ghost girl, paddling away in her airborne coffin keeping an eye on things – the funerary craft turned right serenely heading back east.

Betty felt like waving, shouting out – but she must restrain herself.

CHAPTER

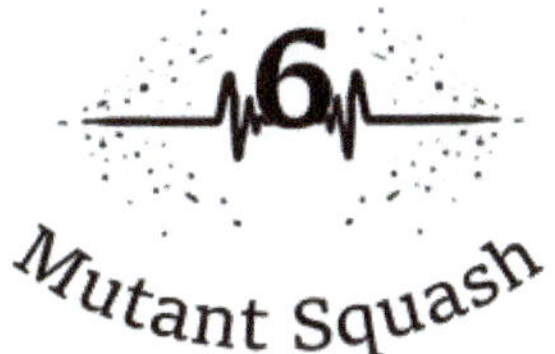

Mutant Squash

he next day was Halloween. Betty came down to breakfast, her head still buzzing from the night before. Herr Bauer and the professor were already sitting at the table being waited on by Netta and Lottie.

"What a pumpkin!" Willi exclaimed to his wife, helping himself to another sausage. "The largest I've ever seen. A true giant! What do you make of that, Netta?"

"How many pies could I bake with it?"

"No, forget the pies! The size of it was incredible, its girth truly tremendous, and there it was, plumb on top of the flat wagon, lording it over everything. It quite took my breath away!"

"An awesome sight," agreed Van Selsing, buttering a slice of rye bread with a knife.

"And as young Zmunxy here says, probably a mutant mastermind, an evil ringleader, a royal bigwig of the pumpkinhead swines. If we could only get a shot at it with a cannon, or tip some harmful chemical agent over it, we'd be laughing, and this curse on our village might get lifted once and for all," said the innkeeper.

"Wishful thinking." The professor was doubtful. "A curse is a curse and will always have serious magical undertones. But yes, perhaps if we pulped this giant pumpkin it might have a positive effect."

"Oh, please save it!" With a squeaky voice, Netta now seemed to be pleading clemency on behalf of the thing. "All that plump cooking flesh mustn't go to waste. I am quite as excited as Willi. You must preserve it and bring it back home to the Block and Stake, whole and in one piece on a cart."

"Don't be so woolly-headed, Netta," the innkeeper said seriously. "This mega-sized autumnal vegetable may have the supernatural capacity to kill us. We just don't know what we're dealing with yet. We're not talking about an ordinary show pumpkin that wins top prize in the marquee, for goodness sake! Fetch us some more of those flavoursome sausages and keep your silly ideas to yourself. We did not risk life and limb last night just for some trite quest to fill a woman's larder so that she can bake pies on an industrial scale."

"By the way," said Betty, tucking into her breakfast of egg and bacon. "I saw Katrina last night on the platform with the other pumpkinheads that arrived on the train. Or at least I recognised her flowery dress and clumpy shoes from my time spent in the railway carriage."

"Yes, of course. Pass me some of that excellent scrambled egg, will you Betty," said Herr Bauer, enjoying his meal and not really that bothered.

Later on, Old Adolf arrived at the Block and Stake and, once settled in his usual fireside chair, ordered a stein, brimful of Weizenbier beer and, after wiping the froth from his lip, offered his own theory on how to destroy this giant pumpkin everyone was going on about.

"The Cross is the only way to defeat these things – the old way is the best, mark you. That one above the fireplace would do fine, or a fancy brass one from the church."

"The old tried and tested method," said Van Selsing. "Certainly, for killing off vampires. One uses melted ingots of silver poured into a special bullet mould and fired from a gun to kill a werewolf, but these pumpkinheads are different."

"Bah! Your mutant, oversized pumpkin wouldn't stand a chance against a good old- fashioned crucifix," said Old Adolf, upending his beer stein and downing the remains of his lager. "It would disintegrate before your eyes."

"I would love to stab Mr Pumpkin with my largest kitchen knife and carve out a big slice of sweet flesh," laughed Netta, winking at Hildegard behind the bar. "And stab him again and again. You men are so complicated sometimes."

"I must confess to something horrible," said Betty, drawing all eyes to her.

"Feel free. The more horrible the better," laughed Herr Bauer, much intrigued by his young friend's admission.

"I did not just see Katrina von Blaufelt on the platform of Heidelwagner station last night. I also saw her outside my bedroom window. The curtains were not drawn properly, and I saw this silhouette of a shape tapping at my windowpane."

"But that's three floors up," pointed out the professor.

"There's no drainpipe to climb and precious little ledge," added Herr Bauer, puffing on his pipe. "No convenient tree branch, either. That really is odd. The girl would be killed if she fell from such a height."

"Well, odd or not, I jumped out of bed and went over to the window. There was her sly laughter, and I knew at once it was Katrina waiting out there for me. 'Von Blaufelt here,' I heard her call from behind the window.

"'Go away,' I said, 'I'm tired.'

"'You're not scared, are you, little girl?'

"No." She was holding a large bag of lemon sherbets, waving it in my face.

"'Let me in, please,' she said gaily. 'And then we can eat and eat so many lovely little sweets. Open the window and you can choose, hee, hee. Our mouths will be smothered in yummy sherbet,'

"For a minute I got brainwashed and found myself twisting the latch and letting Katrina in. Only it wasn't Katrina, but her huge pumpkinhead alter ego squeezing through the opening, her gash-like mouth full of serrated teeth about to eat me."

The professor went white. "A narrow escape then."

Betty nodded.

"Contagion. I suppose enough of these squash enzymes from a single bite could just conceivably  pollute the blood, tilt the balance," said Van Selsing.

"Phew, you're not kidding! I had to act fast, so I grabbed the blanket off my bed and slung it over Katrina's big, round head before bundling her out of the window again, making sure it was tightly shut.

After rechecking the latch, I drew the curtains and went back to bed, but blow me, she was still levitating outside my window, her illuminated pumpkin face staring at me through the curtain material! So, she hadn't taken the hint."

"'Get lost, Katrina!' I shouted. 'Go and annoy someone else for a change!' Then I remembered something important. I scrambled out of bed and started searching everywhere for that giant-sized bag of lemon sherbets in case she'd dropped them when we were fighting. Annoyingly, I could hear her giggling because she hadn't."

"I am reminded of last October when the brothers Klaus and Hermann Listz were mysteriously abducted from their cottage. All we found was a pair of flailing curtains and a wide-open bedroom window," said the professor. "A trail of footprints led up by the gate. These creatures clearly use hypnosis to lure their victims away into the forest. The brothers are beyond help now, of course. As winter progressed, and still no sign, it became increasingly likely we would never see them again except as pumpkinised mutations." Van Selsing brushed cigar ash from his velvet bow tie and grimly raised his glass to his lips. He concluded, "The fate of Joanna Groundberg, Heinz Bergman, Frederik Nansen and Manfred Muller was thus likewise sealed. All of them vanished on Halloween night of last year and now, thanks to young Betty here, we have at least a better understanding of how it was done."

"Well, I think it a fine tale well told."

"It's not a tale, Herr Bauer. It really happened," replied Betty, annoyed by the innkeeper's dismissal of her very real experience.

"Can you say for certain you did not dream it? I mean to say, it's an awfully long way up for a girl to climb to reach your window."

"Katrina von Blaufelt is not a teenager in the normal sense."

"Of course."

"They called such visitations 'ghosts' in my day," said Old Adolf, puzzled by all the fuss.

"Katrina's not a ghost," retorted Betty indignantly. Betty bit her bottom lip — time to shut up. "Forgive me, a ghost is as apt a description as any, Herr Adolf," she relented.

"A dream — dreamt it all," Herr Bauer chuckled. "Too much of Netta's famous turnip pie and the excitement of the railway yard, I expect."

The innkeeper went behind the bar to collect some crates full of empty beer bottles to take down to the cellar, but paused before he went downstairs.

"Netta, did you put anything in that turnip pie? Young Betty seems to be seeing floating pumpkinheads."

"Oh, stop, Willi. Zmunxy's gone into a huff, don't rib her so."

The professor tut-tutted and got up from his fireside chair to stretch his legs.

"Now, now," said the innkeeper, coming back and patting Betty's head fondly. "My dear young lady, the Block and Stake is your home for a fortnight, and Netta and I are delighted to have you. I meant only to point out the possibilities of an overactive imagination as a jest."

"That's it!" Betty jumped up so fast she nearly tripped over the chair leg, her embarrassment forgotten. "How stupid we've been! The answer's been here all along. It's the gruesome inn sign that holds the key."

"What the devil are you on about now?"

"Whereabouts is the historical place of public execution? The one depicted on the Block and Stake sign, Herr Bauer."

"Why, the market square. That's where they used to burn ..."

"Witches ..."

"And execute ..."

"Heretics!"

"Look, it's just too bloodthirsty to go into now," said Herr Bauer, giving his wife an anxious glance. "It's a long, long time ago. The village wanted to forget, pretend like nothing happened – a shameful event in Heidelberger's history. A few bits of parchment documenting the trials of witches, and so forth, are kept at our local history museum. It's all that's left."

"Where is the museum?"

"Just up the road. Herr Van Selsing is its honorary curator. Why?"

"These old bits of parchment, where are they housed?"

"In a wooden box inside the museum's cleaning cupboard," said Van Selsing, frowning intently. "If it's not been chucked out by the cleaners."

"We must try and find them."

"Very well. I'll let us in, but I can't promise this little foray will lead anywhere."

CHAPTER

Curfew Hour

The Chief of Police, Commander Franz Richstein, rose from his chair to address his men of the Heidelberger division in the briefing room of the police station.

He was proud of his rank and the distinguished gold braid epaulettes and ornately spiked helmet that went with it. His uniform trousers were immaculately creased, and his brown boots polished like glass. He was known as a stickler for discipline, and the two words most often used in his vocabulary were 'honour' and 'duty'.

He took no nonsense from anybody, especially the police constables serving under him: the officers who walked the beat, who were in daily contact with the close-knit community that was 'Heidelberger'.

"I want you all to remember," he said, twiddling his moustache, "that tonight is the worst night of the year. We must be always vigilant. You will carry out my orders to the letter. Is that understood?"

"Yes, sir." The assembled officers spoke with one, unified voice that echoed around the briefing room like a loud bark.

"Tonight is ...?"

"Halloween Nacht, sir!"

"The date ...?"

"October 31st!"

"The threat level ...?"

"Maximum!"

"The cause ...?"

"Pumpkinheads!"

"Good. Now, if I may draw your attention to this map on the wall, you will see that I have marked four different locations: the Tabac Shop, Finkelstiltskin – the chocolate confectioner – Frau Hindenburg's Post Office and last but not least, the ladies' outfitters. I have received information of illicit Halloween goods – paper costumes, decorations such as crepe paper witches, ghosts and goblins, Jack o'lanterns, spider webs, moons, stars and Ouija boards – being sold in secret in dark alleys, shop keepers hiding their wares behind their counters or in boxes cleverly disguised as 'tables' to display their other goods. I want all officers to check these business premises because ...?"

"Halloween parties are banned in Heidelberger, sir!"

"Precisely! A complete curfew will come into effect at four o'clock this evening, and not be lifted until six o'clock tomorrow morning...

It is our job to enforce the curfew. No one allowed on the streets after dark, and no horse-drawn carts or vehicles of any kind to park along the High Street. Any questions?"

An officer put up his hand. "Sir, the rules concerning Halloween are clear, what are our powers exactly?"

"Any child caught breaking the curfew will have all sweets, cakes, popcorn and liquorice confiscated, and prohibited to have any of these things for a week after the offence is committed. Parents must comply or will be ordered to attend the police station and pay a substantial fine. Anything else?"

"Sir, there is a silly game involving autumnal apples bobbing in a tub full of water. The idea is that a person ..."

"Yes, I know what you are getting at," said the Chief of Police indignantly. "No parties of any kind. The village hall, incidentally, is locked and boarded up. There will be no repeat performance of last year's attempted revelry by a group of scoundrels. Officers, one and all, I salute you – and good luck! I

will personally promote – and raise the salary tenfold – of any one of you who manages to arrest a pumpkinhead."

The briefing thus ended, and the officers filed out of the bland, sparsely furnished room and put on their helmets ready to start the shift, but the mood amongst the men was hardly heroic. There was none of the usual jokey banter. 'The plodders' were, of course, very vulnerable as they had no protection should a pumpkinhead happen to turn up unannounced.

Pumpkinheads were not in the same category as loutish youths, burglars, shoplifters, or pickpockets. They were of an indeterminate genetic make-up. The best advice had been offered by Sergeant Hauptmann, who had said, "If you see a pumpkinhead on Halloween Nacht, run for your lives."

Old Man Richstein would be tearing his hair out if he knew his force were of a single mind, that to attempt to arrest one of these things was sheer lunacy and frankly not even on the agenda. Better to have a leisurely smoke and sups of brandy – from hip flasks hidden in their uniforms – at intervals during the long night, keeping a low profile. Keep to the shadows, well out of the way, leave things be.

Half an hour later, Officer Strudel came out of Finkelstiltkin's with a bag full of illicit Halloween treats. He had given the proprietor, Frau Snelt, a stern ticking off. He had made a search behind the counter where he had found the hoard. This October, prices for this sort of product had reached unexpected heights.

About to cross the High Street and head back to the police station to deposit the confiscated stash, Officer Strudel noticed something suspicious.

"You!" he called out, running across the cobbles,

alerted by the briefest glimpse of a black, pointed hat and trailing cloak darting down the narrow alley between the Block and Stake Inn and the Post Office. Following the suspect, he barked, "Stop!" in a loud voice. He was gaining ground, the sound of his stomping boots echoing back at him from the steep brick walls on either side of the alleyway.

"No, *you* stop!" The teenage girl turned, pointing her outstretched finger directly at the policeman.

He found himself paralysed on the spot, unable to move a muscle, or even blink.

He saw enough in that brief instant, though. As she scampered off round the corner, he knew what he had just encountered.

It's one of them, he thought, so at least his brain was still computing. Gradually, the pain in his chest subsided, life came back to the traumatised muscles and the blood started to flow again. His temporarily frozen fingers eased their grip on the bag and it fell to the pavement with a distinct 'clump'. He had pins and needles all over, but at least he was okay.

CHAPTER

8

Katrina's Warning

While the others went rushing on ahead, Betty took her time and strolled up the High Street past the quaint 'olde worlde' shops, peering at their gaily-painted fronts.

Houses in the village of Heidelberger were similar to those in most parts of the area – timber-beams, painted shutters, steeply-pitched roofs and gables carved with hearts, doves and royal coats of arms. But more intriguing was the graffiti – strange, disfigured beasts, goblin-like faces and magical symbols cut into the wood to ward off evil, for in these parts, folk were deeply superstitious and crossed themselves at every opportunity.

Betty paused to check out a mouth-watering display of Apple Strudels on offer in the window of Hahn's the baker. The clock tower in the market square could be heard chiming the quarter hour as Frau Hindenburg popped out to greet her, bearing a gift of coinage.

"Thank you," said Betty, slightly taken aback.

"Any friend of Netta Bauer always has a welcome in my heart. Are you going far, dear?"

"The museum, Frau Hindenburg."

"Ach, our museum hosts so many notable artefacts – a spindle, the woodcutter's gloves, hedge cutter's tools, an old kiln, a collection of speckled fowls' eggs, ladies' hats from the seventeenth-century."

Hardly anything to set Betty's pulse racing, but then she was not intending to look nostalgically at old junk all day. "Farewell, Frau Hindenburg."

"Good day, young lady, and enjoy your hour or so spent at our museum finding out about the history of Heidelberger."

"Yes, but not the sort of history you're thinking of!" Betty muttered to herself.

While pausing at the greengrocers to check her red, pillar-box hat, Betty's stomach started to constrict, for, behind her, mirrored in the reflective plate glass, a pretty girl wearing a flowery dress and clumpy, thick-heeled shoes was grinning at her.

"Katrina, what are you doing here?"

Betty turned round to face her, mildly annoyed that she had been surprised like this. "Warning you not to meddle, little girl," she said in a husky voice. "Your fine English ways are not ours. In these parts we have olden rules and we abide by them, and now autumn's here and October with us once more, you would do well to mind your own snotty business so far as us pumpkinheads are concerned. So go away – or join us."

"Not a chance. I like the Bauers and the professor, and why should people in the village have to put up with this curse every Halloween?"

"We're not simply going to turn into mush. You just don't know what you're dealing with. I've tried to be nice so far, but you're just horrible to me."

"Nice? You call trying to scare me last night nice? That was sneaky."

"I only wanted to be your friend and give you a lemon sherbet, like you did."

"And turn me into a mutant – no thanks! Look, I really must be going."

"Where are you hurrying off to now? The sweetie shop?"

"The museum, Katrina."

The girl couldn't believe what she was hearing. "That boring old place? Wait, the big, fat, crawly spiders are nice. Can I come too?"

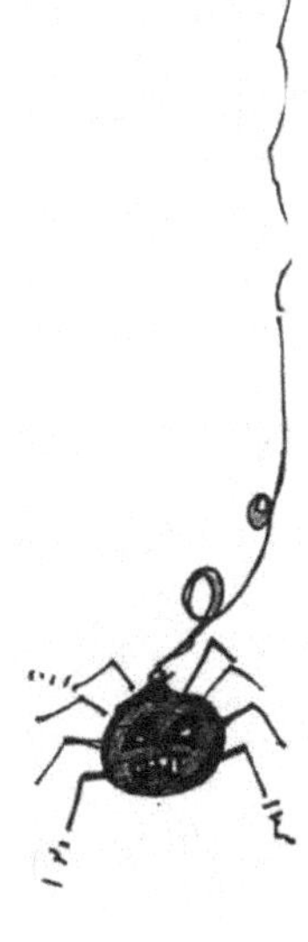

Betty was naturally against this. "Er, no. As a matter of fact, I'm going to study rare fowls' eggs, make a list of them and draw one or two for school," she lied brilliantly.

"Borrring." The mere mention of school made Katrina vanish into thin air. Betty walked on for a bit when, curiously, something small and round, roughly the size of a golf ball, came rolling across the pavement and clunked at her feet.

"A hex!" a woman shrieked, dropping her shopping and burying her face in her hands. Others in the vicinity kept their distance, looking on anxiously, while a brave old gentleman in lederhosen came rushing across and pluckily started stamping on the shrunken pumpkin with his heavy country boots *squashing the squash* until it was no more than messy pulp on the pavement.

"You're safe now." Karloff Schmidt, an old forester, came over to check that Betty was okay. "I'm afraid October's a bad month for evil hexes."

Hardly listening, all Betty could hear were Katrina's clumpy shoes running off into the distance. She got herself together and hurried off to the museum where Herr Bauer was shouting at her to get a move on.

Incredibly, a pair of Bog Common strays – a one-eared, scrawny Alsatian with a gammy eye, manky fur and scars on its muzzle, bald patches from being in fights, and a menacing, growling Collie that bared its fangs in nervous greeting – seemed to take a shine to Betty and impeccably behaved, escorted her the rest of the way. Since going through that old tunnel – strange songs had kept entering her head fully formed. For instance, passing the patisserie:

'Aint make believe

Nor fakery

Goin ta the bakery

Yo – have faith I say

A jam doughnut

Cake on a plate

As stated, I ate it.

CHAPTER

Cursevow

Once inside the museum, the broom cupboard was easy to locate. Amongst the carpet beaters, scrubbing brushes, feather dusters and a variety of powders was to be found the long-discarded cardboard box.

Betty reached into the cleaning cupboard, fumbled about in the box and pulled out a tatty sheet of parchment, yellow and crinkly with age, nibbled by mice. It was headed 'The Curse of Maria Kleinz von Sternberg – being a complete rebuttal of all charges of sorcery laid against her in the year of our Lord 1662'.

"I never thought to look here," admitted Van Selsing, bringing over the desk lamp so that they could read it better. The writing was in old Germanic Lutheran script and the professor did his best to translate:

YOU SHOULD BE THOROUGHLY ASHAMED OF YOURSELF, HERR MAGISTRATE. YOU, MY ONCE TRUSTED FRIEND AND LAWYER, LIKE THE OTHERS, HAVE BETRAYED ME. THIS IS A VILLAGE OF WICKED, SPINELESS VIPERS EAGER TO PROFIT BY DISCLOSING TO CERTAIN INFORMANTS' COMPLETE

UNTRUTHS AND FABRICATED EVIDENCE TO DAMN ME TO THE FLAMES ON ACCOUNT OF A STUPID HAIRY WART AND INGROWN TOENAIL, SO THAT MY WEALTH AND PROPERTY MIGHT BE DISPOSED OF TO YOUR FINANCIAL GAIN. WELL, IF I AM TO BE BURNT AT THE STAKE IN THE MARKET SQUARE ON HALLOWEEN NACHT — OCTOBER 31ST, 1662 — A MUCH TROUBLESOME CURSE WILL FOLLOW FROM THIS TIME FORWARD FOR MANY GENERATIONS TO COME. OH, BY THE BY, AFTER CREMATION, I HAVE REQUESTED MY GOOD FRIEND, PLAIN MRS DALE, TO SCATTER MY ASHES ON MY VEGETABLE GARDEN, WHICH HAS PROVIDED ME WITH SO MANY HAPPY HOURS, FOR THE CULTIVATION OF PRIZE VEGETABLES. THIS SMALL FAVOUR I AM SURE YOU WILL NOT DENY A HARMLESS OLD WOMAN.

YOURS SPITEFULLY, MARIA

"Mein Gott, I think she *was* a witch after all. This explains everything." Herr Bauer sucked on the stem of his empty meerschaum pipe.

"Plain Mrs Dale, eh, spreading her ashes on the vegetable garden, indeed, where Maria no doubt grew her prize pumpkins..."

"But how can we, the village, atone for this centuries-old curse?" asked Van Selsing.

"By planting Maria's giant pumpkin on Holy ground, up by the crossroads."

"The village cemetery?"

"Exactly!"

"But we have to fetch this giant pumpkin first," said Zmunxy, wondering how such a massive vegetable could be shifted – it must weigh a ton!

"The mystery train we saw last night will doubtless be heading our way this evening. We must attempt to unhitch the flat wagon from the rest when it's moving. Maybe those pumpkinheads will be so focused on Halloween that they'll not notice the omission to their ranks and by the time they do...

we'll be on our way to Heidelwagner cemetery to plant it in consecrated ground. The timing will be critical if such a daring plan is to succeed," said the professor, taking out his clay pipe.

"If angry Maria the witch finally decides to relinquish her curse after all these centuries, we'll have done splendidly. But tell me, Herr Professor, which of us is stupid enough to attempt such a suicidal venture? Unhitching the couplings of a flat wagon while the train is in motion is surely extremely dangerous."

"I'll do it," said Betty, full of confidence.

"Me and my friends have helped Mr Nincolme Poopson, the railway signalman where I live in Glim Glumswick, many times."

"Well I suppose," agreed the innkeeper. "Your young, limbs more supple than mine, or the Professor's – but it's still darned risky."

"But if we can get that big squash to the churchyard, the village may be saved," Betty reminded them.

"I know a little stone bridge just outside Heidelwagner. It would only take us five minutes or so to get there."

"We'll need a big cart and help to move it," said Van Selsing earnestly.

"Kurt has the very thing in his yard."

"What about Old Adolf? Is he up for a bit of digging, I wonder?"

"Him and the rest of us. This pumpkin, large and rotund as it is, will require an immense hole to be created."

CHAPTER

10

Black October

The professor was taking time out at home, having spent the best part of an hour clearing leaves and making sure his windfall of bright-red crab apples were collected – Netta used those for jam. He would leave the bruised ones on the ground for birds to peck.

The sweet, nutty smell of smoke from his bonfire drifted across the garden toward the library window. Leaning back in his leather armchair, feet stretched out in front of the fire, he lit his pipe and mulled things through.

Were they being downright foolish, pitting their combined wits against a bona fide witch with a grudge? Yes, they were, but it was too late to care. There could be no turning back.

Unbeknown to the professor, relaxing by the fire, a teenage girl wearing a pointy hat and dark cape was watching the house. She was no merry exponent of trick or treating, which was banned in Heidelberger, however Katrina von Blaufelt was on a mission, she was using her telepathic powers to determine the professor's thoughts, and thereby find out what was going on between that stupid English girl and the others. What scheme were they hatching? Oh, what a stern lesson would be coming sherbet girl's way on this, the best Halloween of all.

While the professor finalised the details of their strategy, Katrina shut her eyes and was aware of a vague image forming in her mind. Again and again, she could visualise some old stone bridge crossing a railway line. She wished herself deeper into the trance-like state and saw a tall pine-needle tree. She instantly recognised the spot – it was situated in part of the forest. Katrina yelped with glee and went running off, her pointy witch's hat held firmly in place with a ribbon tied beneath her chin. Jacob Van Selsing took another puff on his clay pipe. Kurt had offered the use of his huge cart, what a lark it was keeping your true intentions a secret! Willi had muddled through, telling a tale about needing the cart for shifting a load of wood for burning in the massive fireplaces at the Block and Stake during the winter months, which was to be collected from Carlesborgen. Like heck!

Old Adolf needed little persuasion to join the dangerous escapade and gladly agreed to put his skills to the test, the price of compliance being two kegs' worth of best brewed Weizenbier beer.

Jan and Spitzel, the official gravediggers up at the village cemetery, had agreed to turn a blind eye after being paid off in luncheon vouchers. "Just make sure you tidy up behind you," they said.

The doorbell jangled. Van Selsing reached for his cape and wide-brimmed hat and hurried off down the passageway where he kept his winter skis, boots and snowshoes, and where there was a glass cabinet containing various treasured artefacts from his many local history digs, including the village idiot's werewolf skull.

"Ah, Willi," he greeted his old friend with a laugh and a warm hug. "Not bottling out then?"

"You're joking!" insisted Herr Bauer, clapping his gloved hands together, for it was quite cold. "It'd take more than some old witch to scare me away. Betty is making her way to the stone bridge as we speak."

"Bravo, we have the giant pumpkin in our sights then," said the professor, winding a large colourful knitted scarf round his neck.

He gazed across the road at the huge cart, which was now loaded with a heavy, wrought- iron winch pulley that Kurt had also loaned them, an array of oil lanterns, and several spades and shovels.

They both checked their fob watches to make sure they showed exactly the same time, before glancing up at the black October sky, clouds gliding, driving left to right as the east wind blew.

A large gathering of ghosts standing just beyond dimensional vision looked up as well, wondering what there was to see. One scratching his head, the others arms folded or hands raised at waist height in confusion... ghosts don't see what we see you see, and we don't see what they see too.

CHAPTER

Countdown

Old Adolf, it must be said, although keen when asked to help, was not now overly keen to be called away from the comfort of his fireside chair on a night when it was widely accepted as downright dangerous to be outside under the stars. However, it was not dark yet and he must shift his tired bones and get a move on. He drank the remains of his black coffee, and fortified himself with a slug of dry gin, before slinging the old pewter mug in the sink.

"Giant squash indeed!" He, personally, did not believe any of this fairy tale nonsense about a pumpkin. He thought Herr Bauer and the girl, who had been clucking away like a pair of barnyard hens earlier, were most likely exaggerating, or stark-staring bonkers! But if he was to receive a bounty for aiding their ridiculous quest, who was he to argue?

He stooped down and patted the bristly belly of his pet warthog, Frenkel. The lazy pudding lump was snoozing in front of the fire grate, its chubby snout twitching as it dreamed of snuffling for choice truffles.

The old woodcutter reached over and grabbed his crumpled hunting jacket, then, donning his rather tatty and worn flat cap, went outside locking the door to his cottage behind him.

"Ja, still plenty of light," he muttered, checking the winter sky as a flock of crows flew past, the faint grainy outline of the moon beginning to ascend. It so happened that a shortcut led to the crossroads where the public

cemetery was situated, but it wound through the forest for part of the way.

So old Adolf wanted to make good time before it got dark. He glanced at his old fob watch. By now, they would be in position, Willi and the professor walking the horses and cart. It was his allotted task to have a steep-sided trench fully prepared by the time they pulled up at the cemetery gates. According to Herr Bauer, time was of the essence. All of them must pull their weight. There was no margin for error.

All so serious! Trotting along by the post-and-wire perimeter fence that marked the railway, Old Adolf heard the raucous hoot of a train whistle. One of those familiar  engines he had seen hundreds of times was heading his way, and he paused on the leafy bridle path to watch it go past. Mind you, it was a bit of a blur, low-lying mist and clouds of locomotive steam billowing across the fence made it difficult to determine more than the shadowy shapes of the luggage coach and standard carriages. But he got a shock when he viewed a large, round object secured to the flat wagon taking up the rear.

As the train's red tail-lamp disappeared into the distance, he crossed himself several times and had to admit he was wrong – the giant pumpkin was real after all. This daring escapade he was taking part in mattered. He felt humbled, and at the same time a surge of pride flooded through him. What he was about to do counted!

Forgetting the train, now on its way to the stone bridge, he crashed through the trees, shadows of

ghosts darted from his path. He was acutely conscious that he must reach the cemetery before dark, before losing the last vestiges of daylight as that bright All Hallows moon finally held sway over the forest.

He chuckled to himself, thinking what Police Chief Richstein would make of all this. Everyone in the village was meant to be safely locked indoors, obeying the curfew. Well, not him, and to think he was over eighty years of age and still game enough for this little jaunt! Admittedly, his spindly legs were getting a bit bowed and infirm, and he would suffer pain in his joints later, but that didn't matter. So far, so good, he had not been accosted by any pumpkinheads lurking in the bushes and was now walking at a reasonable pace along the main road.

He could see the cemetery gates up ahead, cast in wrought iron, with the ugly carved gargoyles squatting on top of pillars either side.

The gates remained unlocked, so anyone was free to enter or leave at whatever hour they chose. Old Adolf, who was beginning to feel his age, lingered a while to catch his breath, then, crossing the gravel drive, stumbled up the grassy slope to where the gravediggers' hut and storage shed were discreetly situated behind a tall, slatted fence. All the paraphernalia for funerals was kept up there: tools, grave boards and massive shovels used for earth clearance and filling in the graves after the mourners had left.

Granted, the chilly October air, the cloying damp of autumn, the gloomy vista of ivy-clad vaults, lichen-stained monuments and headstones and crosses, did not exactly inspire him to burst into song, but there were compensations. He wetted his lips, slid back the shed doors, and loaded up with all the tools he required.

CHAPTER

12

The Bridge

The narrow cinder trail led from the village, winding through the forest to the little used, stone-built bridge used by trekkers. It crossed the line on a straight stretch of track and was ideal as a vantage point for judging the speed and distance of any approaching train.

So how fast did a pumpkinhead train actually travel? Well, Betty thought a justified comparison could be made to the volks electric trains that trundle slowly along Brighton seafront from the Aquarium station to Black Rock.

Anyhow, the flat wagon was coupled a good distance from the cab, with the luggage van and two passenger carriages in between, so Betty should be able to jump aboard relatively safely if timed and judged well.

The afternoon light was fading, and in not long the pumpkinhead special from Heidelwagner would be trundling under the bridge on its way to the village.

When Betty left Glim Glumswick to holiday in Heildeberger, she hadn't prepared for such expeditions as this – her shoes and clothes were certainly not suitable for jumping onto moving trains, however slowly they were going. Herr Bauer and his wife Netta had very kindly requisitioned some clothes more suitable for the occasion, including some very rough canvas breeches and heavy, somewhat cumbersome boots. Betty hurriedly tied her hair back with a length of ribbon, thus reducing the risk of getting her long, wavy locks entangled in any mechanical contraptions she may come across.

Kurt had kindly loaned a stout rope that she was to use to slide down onto the train.

Betty judged the trains along here travelled an average of five miles an hour, little more than the pace of a horse-drawn carriage, so that when she launched herself onto the moving train, this should be no more dangerous than some of the games that she and her best friends back home in Glim Glumswick sometimes played. 'Deer stalker', in particular, often resulted in injured parties as two of them lurched around the playground blindfolded trying to catch each other.

Down below, beside the steps leading onto the bridge, she heard the crackle of leaves, the snap of twigs and thought she saw a flash of orange moving behind a mass of tangled gorse. Maybe she was mistaken, maybe it was a wild boar, or something, snuffling about for acorns. A ghost? No.

She soon forgot, looped her rope round the most central parapet and, as she was tying a knot, she thought about her mother and Aunt Medley back home and hoped they had got the letter she had sent.

"Boo! Tee-hee-hee!"

A shock wave rippled from Betty's boots up through her spine, striking the nape of her neck.

"Ahh – you scared me!"

She twisted round to find who else but Katrina, standing on the bridge leering at her, her pearly white teeth criss-crossing each other in loathing – but she was good at keeping up a pretence.

"I've a game for you, a kind of 'look about' game. Stop what you're doing and climb onto one of those stone blocks. I want to show you an owl's nest. The only way to see them is by climbing up onto that ledge, then you can tell me how many you can see in the tall tree."

"No, I will not, you skilamalink!" replied Betty. "That's a trick, not a treat. You're going to tie my boot laces together, or something, and push me off."

"So what!" Katrina said nastily. "We've all had enough of your nosy delving, and Mother wants you dead."

"Mother? Whose mother?"

"All of ours mother."

"Eh?" Betty was confused.

"Maria Kleinz von Sternberg, silly. You read about her at the museum."

"Oh, the witch!"

Katrina grimaced. "She's not a witch, that's a poisonous old toothless haggy name. Don't call her a witch. She's a beautiful sorceress!" All of a sudden, Katrina's face ballooned out, her skin stretched first, turning green and then pinky orange, her teeth becoming larger and more jagged, her eyes hollow pools of lantern light that threatened her. "You and those grown-ups are in big trouble. Halloween is not the time to be messing with Maria."

She – or it – let out a hiss of chilly vapour and ran off. Betty soon lost sight of her. A loud train whistle blew along the railway line – she prepared herself and crouched behind the parapet.

CHAPTER

Since her ashes had been scattered over the original plant centuries before, the witch's spirit somehow inhabited the round, fleshy autumn fruit. Those blessed with psychic vision would, in fact, have been able to see Maria as in life – a buxom, handsome woman wearing traditional costume for the period, but no pointy hat or broomstick for which she had no need.

She sat happily inside the glowing, warty-skinned receptacle. As it became darker outside, the pumpkin lit up more brightly, and so her lovely smile increased. But this October, she sensed trouble. Determined minds, including a foreign girl's, were matched against hers, and unfortunately, pumpkinheads were, to put it kindly, a bit empty-headed.

The round-faced driver of the train peered from his cab. He saw the stone bridge up ahead. He had seen the bridge many times before and found it unremarkable.

A bit further up the line was the works depot, used by maintenance staff for basic storage of fence posts, rolls of wire and wooden sleepers. He found this unremarkable also and would barely notice – which was extremely lucky! For at that moment, a large horse-drawn cart, loaded with a winch pulley, was being manoeuvred into the depot, concealed mostly by trackside undergrowth.

A misty haze of locomotive smoke drifted along by the trees as the light engine passed under the bridge. No one had so far seen Betty dangling over the bridge on the other side.

Swiftly help was at hand for Tudor Sefton came gliding down in her flying coffin – able to expertly manoeuvre the craft into hover mode, easing it gently closer to the bridge parapet, from there Betty clambered aboard – settling herself by the lantern stick. Within seconds piles of sooty locomotive smoke had engulfed the pair – making Betty sneeze.

"Chase that weird train," Zmunxy told her friend – "go get it gal – catch up so I'll be able to leap onto the rear wagon"

"Rightho - I can see, buffers and the tail headlight wotsits." Tudor went into overdrive with her paddle, making the coffin hurtle along through the air, twirling it round – a large gathering of ghosts flocking to view the pumpkin heist, wildly applauding Tudor Sefton's deft use of her paddle before dissolving in that way that they do..

At the right moment Betty jumped and hurtled downwards, amazingly landing on both feet and managing to grab hold of a convenient handrail as the flat wagon travelled along.

No one saw her jump, that is apart from Maria, sitting in her pumpkin throne-room. She watched, aghast, as the teenager calmly unhitched the coupling and the rest of the train went steaming on ahead without her.

The pumpkinheads crammed into the carriages were oblivious to the hijack of their giant pumpkin.

When the flat wagon eventually squealed to a halt, with Betty leaning her full weight against the rusty brake handle to stop the thing, they were somewhere along a forested section with a tall post-and-wire fence looming beside the track.

A large, horse-drawn cart came out of nowhere and backed up to the fence. The lanky figure of Van Selsing, cloaked and wearing his wide-brimmed hat, leapt up to operate the winch pulley. The task of transferring the giant pumpkin had begun.

A few of the ghosts made up an audience at the treeline nearby, deep in animated discussion about events so far and those yet to unfold.

Before they had secured the straps around the pumpkin, Maria invisibly flew out of her pumpkin, causing a flourish of autumn leaves to hurtle about the tracks in a spiral pattern.

Oh, what is to happen to 'old faithful'? she wondered, watching from above. Without her pumpkinheads, she could never physically intervene, but she could still, if she wanted, turn them all into a lot of frogs. But she was impressed with the girl's derring-do, so she decided against spells – *for the time being*. The winch raised the cumbersome vegetable over the wire fence and swung it onto the back of the cart.

In no time, the horses were hauling the cart to the leafy cemetery at a steady canter, Maria flying above, easily able to keep up.

CHAPTER

The cart pulled up just inside the cemetery gates.

"How goes it, Adolf?" shouted Herr Bauer, patting the horses in gratitude for their hard work. Hauling this massive cart loaded with the very weighty pumpkin and pulley had certainly been a strain on them. Adolf had been digging away relentlessly for the last half an hour and was kept motivated by the reward awaiting him.

"Ach, you know how it is, Willi. A keg or two of good old Weizenbier keeps us old foresters happy," he chuckled, peering ahead like some wizened gnome. "Soon be able to plant that tremendous pumpkin of yours. What a whopping fellow he is. I see you were not exaggerating, Herr Bauer. The seeds must be the size of coconuts."

"You've earned your kegs, Adolf, but I fear there's a witch about, so let's get a move on and finish the job."

Van Selsing rolled up his sleeves and stooped his tall, ungainly frame to begin shovelling earth onto the already mountainous pile. Betty joined him, at first scanning the sky above the fir trees for a witch on a broomstick as in fables. But all she could see were clusters of brightly-lit stars.

Invisible, Maria flew – never on a broomstick – by 'astral free flying', an even better way of getting about and more refined and ladylike than an old hazel stick.

"Drat!" Maria cursed, landing like a feather on top of a stoney 'hair do' belonging to the smooth, white marble head of the one-time Mayor of Heidelberger – Franz Joseph Brandt.

"A village cemetery by the crossroads is classed as hallowed ground."

This meant that Betty and the rest were protected against any nasty spells she might feel inclined to sling their way.

Everything was now ready – Herr Bauer rushed across to fetch the horses and cart. He led the horses across the grass, strewn with leaves, careful to avoid crashing into any stone ornaments.

The sorceress hopped from the marble Mayor to the stone effigy of a grim-faced head postmaster, to the pompous statue of a former brewer magnate, down onto a far less grand wooden cross. She was seething mad that her 'old faithful', as she liked to call it, was about to be planted in consecrated ground where the pumpkin's flesh would soon rot and be consigned to the elements from whence it came, and her power to invoke a curse on the village would be gone with it.

With all four hauling on the chains of the pulley, they managed to lift the giant pumpkin above the hole, but it was when Herr Bauer's hands slipped off the taught chain that a hitch took place.

Betty, Van Selsing and Adolf, try as they might, could not hold the strain long enough for Herr Bauer to recover and regain his grip. Suddenly, they could feel the chain rapidly slipping through their hands and had to let go, and a splatty sound was heard as the out-of- control pumpkin hit the bottom.

Like a Greek chorus the onlooking ghosts cupped their mouths with their hands.

Glowing with a weaker translucence than before, the thick, warty skin of the pumpkin became increasingly cracked, fissures tearing open, revealing bright orange, spongy flesh.

Old Adolf, as aged as he was, hurriedly grabbed the huge shovel and tipped scoopful after scoopful of earth on top of it, working relentlessly, not stopping until the pumpkin was buried — he even levelled the top soil, hitting it down hard to make a tidy job of it.

Maria Kleinz von Sternberg, when faced with the fact that the enchanted, centuries-old pumpkin was doomed, had to admit defeat, and after so long a time, the curse of the village was finally lifted.

The audience of ghosts relieved, wiping brows and smiling with relief.

The pumpkinhead train never arrived that All Hallow's Eve, it simply vanished, taking its passengers with it. But the dark magic of Halloween made something of a resurgence when they drove back along the forest road that night.

Sinister spherical shapes with triangular eyes and gashes full of jagged teeth appeared in the branches of trees, aglow with malignant radiance, and some of these would, from time to time, come crashing down as they rode along, exploding in a mush of orange pulp, sending streaks of the stuff into the cart.

Was Katrina von Blaufelt amongst them? Young Betty shuddered to think. She tried to convince herself that she had seen the last of the clumpy-shoed girl of the forest. But she did have a habit of popping up when you least expected her, so she was a bit edgy for the rest of the journey.

CHAPTER

There had been a 'tip-off', somebody had told the station sergeant on desk duty that "the cemetery had been invaded – lanterns aglow, digging and crashing sounds, horses snorting and neighing. Hadn't they, the police, better see what was going on? After all, it was hardly conducive to a good night's sleep!"

"Officer Strudel!" the desk duty sergeant called out. "You and Weiss, get over to the cemetery immediately – complaint of vandals. Gottit?"

Weiss froze. His bushy hair seemed to rise up. He suddenly looked very pale and meek.

"The cemetery, Sergeant?" he gulped. "Might I remind you, sir, that firstly it is a full moon and that secondly it is... it is Halloween?"

"And you are a subordinate officer who takes orders from me and therefore does as I say. Now, get off your backsides and stop acting like a pair of silly, scared spinsters – or I'll report you both to the old man."

Weiss didn't want to go out, and neither, for that matter, did Officer Strudel. His duty roster had been so well organised until Sergeant Foche came on shift. Earlier, he had deposited his bag of illegal treats that had been on sale under the counter at Finkelstiltskin's, and had been commended highly for his handling of the incident. Then, due to his fragile state of mind, after being zapped by a suspected pumpkinhead in the alley along the High Street, he had been assigned general station duties – paperwork, filing of forms, looking after the cells.

Nothing too hectic, or demanding.

Strudel glanced at the wall clock above the desk. A quarter past twelve – so it was gone midnight, at least, and the woodland could be avoided if they ran along the road.

He stubbed out his cigarette and followed Weiss out of the station. Round the back was just the same as at the front. The village police station was a square concrete building, depressingly bereft of trees, plants, grass or flower boxes. Plain and functional,

architecturally inept, like the place was designed to be a zoo enclosure.

"Mein Gott, just our luck!" moaned Weiss.

"Sent into the heart of darkness, a place of cannibals and spectres and ghouls. It had to be the cemetery. Curse whoever went to the station and complained. They should be reprimanded harshly. Don't they realise it's Halloween and that pumpkinheads could be about?"

They hurried along the road towards the cemetery seeing nothing out of the ordinary on their way. Soon they arrived at the cemetery gates.

"Can't see any lights," shouted Strudel, "nor hear any voices. Place seems deserted."

"Glad to hear it," said Weiss, "Just the once round to check and then it's back to the station."

The wrought-iron gates swung open and the two police officers trudged up the sweeping drive used by hearses and mourners' carriages. The way was lined with white marble angels and statues of pompous old brewery magnates, judges, mayors, post office officials and other notables of Heidelberger from the past.

"Oh, I don't believe in ghosts, of course," mumbled Weiss, patting his truncheon. "But a churchyard at night is still a creepy place. I mean, you hope to hell that those who lie beneath – the dead, that is – are behaving themselves and not about to ..."

At that moment a kindly ghost gent pulled a yew branch out of his way with a smile and theatrical bow, preventing it from catching on his face in the dark.

"Shush!" Officer Strudel said, directing his colleague's gaze to a patch of ground over by the stone-clad wall. "What in heaven's name have the gravediggers been up to?"

The police officers traipsed across the well trodden grass to where horse and cart tracks were clearly discernible, rutted into the mud.

"Have they buried an elephant here?" Weiss scratched his head, totally bemused. "The plot's so large. Were they starting a construction of some sort, I wonder?"

"Shall we report it?"

"Nah, too much bother. I'm sure the parson knows about this. It's the gravedigger's business, not ours. If they want to work late, so what? Vandals! What vandals?"

Both men burst out laughing. The relief was palpable. There were no youths loitering about, or groups of vagrants, or a sinister drunk lurking behind a tomb.

They had checked and were satisfied that, apart from cart tracks and footprints scattered about, no law had been broken, or offence been committed against persons or property. Time to leave, get back to the station.

As they stepped outside the gates there was an immense flash of light, a popping sound and all the graves lit up. Where once had stood the two police officers was now a pair of toads croaking to one another, still trying to keep up a conversation.

Unfortunately for Weiss and Strudel, Maria the witch was about, keen to keep her hand in by trying out one of her spells, because it was still officially Halloween and witches everywhere were celebrating.

The kindly ghost gent, arms folded, looked on while slowly shaking his head and burst into a rap song.

Ghosts aint edifyin

Loads of the deadified

Along fo' the ride

One on one

Makes me run

Faraslcangit...

CHAPTER

16

Last Train Out

Netta, stirred the coffee pot next morning, while Fraulein Lottie served guests in the breakfast room with a hearty meal, "Shame on you all," she said, "Poor Mr Pumpkin should have been brought back to the inn for me to deal with. I should have carved slices out of him royally for the pantry and sold my pies all over England. My name would have been associated with good eating and I, a firm favourite with the bank managers."

"Oh, do leave off," winked Herr Bauer to Betty. "It'd weigh a ton and never fit into your kitchen, and as for that canny witch I told you of, who nurtured it, why, she'd probably have set the place on fire and blown up your precious oven and hanged poor Lottie upside-down in a tub full of cheese-curd, just for the fun of it."

"It was holy ground that was her final undoing, and now, you see, it protected us against her rage and spell making," said the professor, helping himself to more pickled eggs and sour cream, heaping the concoction onto his plate.

"The pumpkinheads would have tried to shield Maria's pumpkin from harm," said Betty, placing a dollop of jam on her black bread.

"Quite so. The girl's right. All hell would have broken loose if we'd brought the pumpkin back here. Believe me, Netta, you're better off without that enormous pumpkin. We all are. Save your precious carving knife for chopping up swedes, beets and turnips for today's lunch."

"And did you see Katrina?" Lottie wanted to know, pouring out more coffee. "Did she say hello to your friend, the forest girl?"

She nudged Netta and whispered something — either these women were incredibly naïve or having a laugh at her expense. Betty saw where this was ultimately leading and tried to put a firm stop to it — without success.

"Yes, she dropped in on me last night when I was waiting for the train to come along."

"What?" Lottie looked horrified.

"Why won't you listen? Katrina is a pumpkinhead, not an ordinary girl who goes to school, studies and plays music, so please stop trying to make me be friends with her."

"But if only you'd just talk to her, be nice, be

reasonable."

Lottie and Netta just had no idea – they just didn't get it.

For the rest of the morning, after borrowing Karl Bauer's bicycle, Betty went for a ride in the woods, joined by Lottie who knew all the trails.

A gust from the funnel,

Yo – rumblin' fru

The tunnel

But you gotta be careful

Git out when you outta

The tunnel is a portal

The song of the magical tunnel was calling

The woodland round Heidelberger looked beautiful at this time of the year – trees alive with autumnal colours, the trail covered in a springy mat of nut-bronzed, red and golden leaves.

Suddenly, she became quite still, aware of a strange pull to her inner being, the portal was calling her, Betty must on no account ignore this call – she sensed – the one and only link to her proper world, the special train was due in a little while. The feeling passed - Beyond the stone trekkers' bridge where Betty had launched herself onto the flat wagon, the forest became less well-signposted, and it would be easy to lose one's way if it was not for a guide.

Fortunately, Lottie was a local girl, born and bred, who knew the region well. Even so, Betty got confused a couple of times and took the wrong turning and was finding it difficult to keep up, so it was something of a relief when Lottie called out, "Oh my, just look at this, Betty."

Lottie had, quite by chance, stumbled on a woodland clearing surrounded by pines. Facing them was a straw-fattened, crow- pecked scarecrow with a creepy stitched grin and drawn-on, malevolent-looking eyes that seemed to follow you around. It had a sign strung around its scrawny, broom-handle neck.

"What's it say?" asked Betty, intrigued.

"Well," said Lottie, translating from German into English. "Most odd, I'm afraid, but trust me, it's what it says here." She gave a polite little cough. "'The graves of the fallen – warriors all!'"

Before them was stretched out, not lines of granite headstones or wooden crosses like in a cemetery, but row upon row of ripening pumpkins.

"Crikey! Maybe the pumpkinheads that got destroyed last night are buried here," said Betty in disbelief.

The neat rows of pumpkins were cultivated in richly manured soil.

Who could be the secret gardener? Was the witch, Maria von Sternberg, responsible for spiriting the dead pumpkinheads to this place of war graves last night? Questions needed answering.

Betty trudged along one of the pumpkin rows, getting her shoes muddy and clothes dirty from splashes of manure. The eyes of the straw scarecrow seemed to be watching her every move. She approached a water tap nailed above a tank swimming with green algae. The tap dripped continuously, which was wasteful, so Betty decided to turn it off – only she turned it the way. Instead of water gushing out, she got zapped by a voice she knew only too well, speaking to her directly.

"Hi, it's me... Katrina. We've got plenty of surprises planned for next Halloween. Will you come back and visit our lovely forest next year, Betty?"

"Er, I'll think about it," she stuttered, quickly twisting the tap tightly shut, severing the connection and hurrying back to where Lottie was choosing a pumpkin to take back to Netta's kitchen.

"What about this beauty?" she laughed.

"It will make a lovely pie."

"No, leave it where it is!" pleaded Betty, hustling her away. "Let's get out of here – that scarecrow's really spooking me."

A swishing noise audible only to animals and birds heralded an incoming Tudor Sefton who performed a tricky landing – her flying coffin able to slip along on a carpet of moist autumn leaves bouncing a bit, before coming to rest at the edge of the pumpkin field.

Zmunxy hurried over.

"Did you like your Halloween experience this year Betty?"

"Rather – beats trick n' treating, Fairy tale Heidelberger was a real gas Tudor, but I don't fancy missing my last train and ending up in Halloweenland for ever." The girl laughed, accepting a paddle while hopping in, going off with Tudor for a quick spin around Bog Common and the village rooftops.

Characters in the series

The Fairytale Detective Series

Halloweenland

Betty's Chronicles of Glim Glumswick

Betty – more of the Fairytale Detective

www.ingramcontent.com/pod-product-compliance
Lightning Source LLC
Chambersburg PA
CBHW061219210726
48294CB00006B/1905